LET IT BLEED

Nicole Nesca

By Nicole Nesca

The Sexual Repression Collection
Kink
Canned
Kamikaze White Noise (An Anthology)
Diamond Scarred Alley
Let It Bleed

Copyright © 2017 Nicole Nesca

ISBN: 978-1-7752112-4-2

All rights reserved

Printed in The United States of America

Published by -

Screamin' Skull Press

screamingskullpress.net

There is nothing to writing. All you do is sit down at a typewriter and bleed.

Ernest Hemingway

This is a work of fiction -

LET IT BLEED

Hemorrhaged

After several days of not being able to bend over thus making me unable to shave my legs, I stepped into the shower. Happy. Happy that I was finally able to bend over and shave my legs after what seemed like an eternity. It was really only a couple of weeks. A couple of weeks since my hysterectomy. I was still dealing with the psychological ramifications of this surgery, but dealing quite nicely.

Feeling good for the first time in a couple of days, I stepped into the shower. Ready to feel better. To feel "normal". Ready to move on. I turned on the water. It was warm and refreshing and felt good. I turned to put my head under the water and I felt a cramp in my lower abdomen. With my eyes closed, I continued to wet my hair. I felt a hot sensation begin to tun down my inner thighs. I opened my eyes and saw blood running from between my legs. Large amounts of blood. I turned the shower off and grabbed a towel and placed it between my legs. Still in shock, I began to yell for my sleeping husband. Afraid to move and afraid to yell any louder, I could feel the blood running out of me with every heart beat. Terrified, I crawled to the phone to call my mother-in-law who was staying upstairs. She answered and I told her I needed help and to please come down the stairs. She ran down the stairs and found me in the kitchen. Naked and clutching a towel between my legs. There was a trail of blood from the shower to the kitchen floor. I started to feel drowsy. I asked her to wake-up my husband. She did. She told him to dial 9-1-1. She helped me to dress and to breath and calm down. There was so much blood. Ziggy, my husband, entered the kitchen sleepy-eyed and looked into the shower before he was told to dial 9-1-1 again. He did.

Two minutes later, an ambulance and the fire department showed at my front door. I was wearing a bath towel under my sweat pants and hobbled to the ambulance while my family was answering all of their questions. I could hear the sirens over head as they rushed me to the emergency room of the hospital where my surgery took place. I was terrified and trying to remain conscious. I was afraid to stop talking. Afraid to move and afraid I was dying. My blood pressure kept dropping and I was running a fever. I wasn't in any pain, which was more frightening than the blood loss. My husband sat in the front seat with the driver. I couldn't hear or see him but I knew he was there. I just kept talking. About the weather. About the neighborhood. About anything. Trying to stay awake.

When I reached emergency, I waited in a hall while they readied a room for me. I told the nurse that I was bleeding and that I needed a pad. She brought me a pantyliner. I told her I need a bigger one. I inched my way onto an exam table and waited. I could feel the blood moving out of me. I felt extremely cold and sleepy. I answered every question. There were so many people and yet, no one examined me. They never peeked under the gown. Question after question. Face after face. My daughter and my husband were finally allowed into the room. My mother-in-law, aunt and uncle were allowed in to visit me. I started hyperventilating. I could feel my life slipping away. I felt pain and I felt weak. I was crying but there were no tears. Panic set in. I started demanding to see a doctor. She ordered a bedside ultrasound. She examined me and asked for a family and surgical history. I answered her questions. The tears came. The pain came. The exam came. The morphine came.

My heart rate began to raise as my blood pressure was falling. The morphine was a welcomed reprieve from the moments. The moments that lead me to this place. I felt no pain. I felt the tears run down my cheeks and yet I couldn't feel myself cry. I was talking but the words were unintelligible. I think I was laughing and crying and praising Keith Richards all in the same breath. I felt I was dying. I kept talking. I kept talking. I could not stop moving and squirming on the table. More doctors came. Two IV lines were placed and I was still in the emergency room. I kept trying to keep my eyes open so that I could see my daughter and my husband and my family. I didn't want to close my eyes. I was afraid they wouldn't open again. I am not sure how long I was there. There was no time. No window. Just more and more faces and more and more questions. The ER doctor paged surgeons and specialists. I was examined more and more and more. There was more morphine. More tears. More laughter. More hallucinations. My husband could not look anywhere but into my eyes. After I was examined, poked and veined, there was blood. Blood on the sheets, blood on the bed and blood on the floor. And, no answers. I was admitted for observation. Once I reached my room, twelve hours later, I sent my husband home. Home for some rest. I sent him home and allowed my eyes to close.

Nurses sat next to me in the room and monitored my vitals. I had a rising heart rate and blood pressure that continued to fall. I was asked to stand and blacked out. I fell asleep instantly and was awakened by the on-call surgeon. She told me I had to phone a family member because I had to have surgery again. I was very ill and they needed to find out why. She had blonde hair and blue eyes like my mother. I think I trusted her. I had to trust her. I phoned my husband whom I just sent home and told him he had to come back. They were sending me into surgery right away. I told him not to worry and I told him ow much I loved him. After I hung up, I phoned my mother in Ohio. I told her not to worry and that I would have my husband phone her. It was 10PM in

Winnipeg. 11PM in Ohio. My head was foggy and I couldn't focus and I couldn't keep my eyes open anymore. As they wheeled me into the operating room, I struggled to look at the ceiling. I looked into the light and answered their questions. I watched the mask cover my mouth and nose and breathed deep. I waited a few seconds and then there was nothing.

Dark.

I had another five-hour surgery. I had 1.5 liters of blood and infection removed. I had a slow bleed repaired and adhesions removed from my bowels. I don't remember much else from that night. My husband was there. Tired and worried. I sent him home promising to phone in the morning. I slept. I morphine-slept for a few hours. The next morning, the surgeon came in, early. She explained everything to me with her blonde hair and blue eyes. I wanted to cry but there were too many people around. I was still not allowed to eat and in shock. I waited for another CAT scan to verify that I still had a large hematoma. I did. I moved through the days hooked to morphine and hooked to antibiotics, still in shock. Still high on morphine and still unable to cry. Too many people around. I received two bags of blood and I received more drugs. I was not allowed to go home for seven days. I was in pain on day six and refused the morphine. I started shaking in between doses and was more afraid of that than the pain. The hospital gave me as much as I wanted for as long as I wanted. I let them poke and prod and inject and remove. I watched the walls and listened to people talk. I listened but I could hear them. Family and friends came in and out. Doctors and nurses came in and out. I could hear women and men crying down the hall. All hours of the day and night. I could see women with no hair carrying poles as they shuffled down the hall. Women who were pregnant, women who had lost their children, their organs and some their lives. I could hear them crying. I still couldn't cry. I would wait until everyone was asleep and I would begin my late-night shuffle up and down the halls. I would stare into the night through a window at the end of the hall, watching the cars move back and forth through the night. I waited to feel better and I waited to cry.

The tears didn't come for a week. I phoned my father to tell him what happened. And, they started. Once I started crying, I hung up the phone and laid on my couch and cried for an entire day. I slowly began to walk more. I weaned myself off the pain meds, and I started to realize that I was alive. I was going to be "okay" again.

I still can't take a shower if I am the only one home. I still have nightmares about bleeding. I still look down when I am in the shower. I am six months removed from the hemorrhage. Let it bleed.

Nephew

The combination of curiosity and fever brought me to Youtube.

Typing in your name, I found you.

Years upon years have removed me from your life.

Family struggle and strife.

I last saw you as an addicted, premature birth.

Asked to take you, I refused.

Reasons, only you will ever hear.

I will live with that.

You are much taller and much older.

Much healthier.

More privileged.

Are you more loved?

I live with this.

Do you?

What have you been told?

Will your future story include me?

Who will make the choice this time.

Child

"You cannot stop now."

Watch the sun come up.
    (wherever you may be)
That chip on your shoulder is inherited.
Your jaw-line is mine.
    (so too is the dark)
Those broad shoulders and "come-hell or high-water" eyes
    Are "ours", as well.
Shooting the blind-man, is no win.
    (That's the coward's way)
You know everything that you need to know.

I will stand and wait.

    I will answer for the rest.

        Use the hurt to motivate.

            Move in any direction.
                Just, don't stand still and
    stay…
                    like us.

Should we all "let it be"?

The world is on fire.
Liberals afraid to speak,
Tongue –tied and twisted with the idea of freedom.
    (free-speech no longer exists)
Writers and artists afraid.
    (shiver in the dark)
Should we all "let it be"?
When will we all stop being afraid?
When will we see freedom for all?
Who will answer for our ignorance?
    Our fear?
    Our sorrow?
Hold on tight to your freedoms,
    for they will cease to exist,
        if we continue in silence.

Je Suis Charlie!

February

ice in the trees

air

heavy fog

breathe

tragically beautiful

argumenta

I punched you twice
        in the jaw

you took me
        I tumbled to the floor

on top of me...

you never hit me back

apologies

you slept

phone rang

car-accident

death kissed,
        HER fore-head

and, I knew...
        nothing would ever be the same.

gripped in my arms was the changeling's madness.
I'm never going away.

Holding the mirror

twisted,
tongued viper speaks
rambling thoughts hiss
tears must be cried
heart must beat
      (tom tom tom tom)
you like this shit.
don't you?
can't stop now
you've gotta hold on
can't let go
you prefer those who
      scream when they burn.

Get loud

this better get loud
I've grown tired of the quiet
silence sickens me
things feel too small
      contained
          sealed for freshness and taste
          bubble wrapped minds and hearts
big sky
big schemes
big ideas
big screams

trees whisper thoughts
      maybe dreams
where is reason?

I wonder and I wander towards the east

this better get loud
this better get loud
this better get loud

bring back the colour to my dreams

"silence like a cancer….grows."

The Hangers-On

you hitched a ride to my star
my spirit is in the air
       (I'm nowhere)
redeem your ticket for a later ride
there is nowhere left for me to take you
       you're on your own, now
there are no rules
barnacle friend,
       scrape thee from my hull
i am no longer your Eddie to your Andy
trampled under foot,
       leave.
to continue with you,
       I'd be a fool.
exorcised….
       pure as the driven snow.

NEXT!

YOU AIN'T A BEAUTY. BUT, HEY, YOU'RE ALRIGHT

It was a crisp afternoon in the Mahoning Valley. Most people our age were busy studying for SAT exams. Nichole and me were too busy trying to relax. The future was something that belonged to other girls. Between the two of us, there were two pregnancy scares in the last three months. Enough for one entire lifetime. Nichole and me were dreamers and smart girls. With a little encouragement and dreaming on our (collective) parents minds, we could have been a couple of Steven Hawkins, Einstein types. That didn't exist in the valley. It was just how it was. Both of our fathers worked at the local GM assembly plant in good ol' Lordstown, Ohio. We had a car. It was mine. A '78 Cutlass Supreme. It was midnight blue and silver. I had an 8 track, radio and pull out cassette player. I was proud of my original baby blue faux suede interior. Kregar chrome wheels…it was a ride. Problem was, I couldn't handle my party favors, so, Nichole always had to drive "jezebel" for me. Truth be told, the car was mine in theory but actually belonged to Joe. Me boyfriend at the time.

Anyways, Nichole and I embraced the beautiful fall day and grabbed a couple of country girls from our class. Amy and Maggie. We headed to the country. Can't quite recall the town name, maybe Southington. We stopped for a couple packs of cigarettes and some Little Kings malt liquor. The usual. We were a group of pretty young things jamming to some classic rock on Y-103 (local station). We was born in the USA. Free, working middle class, Sunday school survivors and eighteen years old. The world was our clichéd oyster. Too much to talk about and too much to do to be tied to a desk in class learning how to type wills and papers for a future corporate big wig. We were tired and bored and even more tired and bored with ourselves. Amy was a bit of a hell raiser. We all were, but she had that spark and come-hither glance that opened doors that we had only talked about. (That's how we got the beer.)

We drove out to the corn fields of Columbiana County and parked. It was fun to just be away. None of us had more than a part time job and some familial responsibilities. Take trash out, clean room, etc. We had families, sure, but they were all too wrapped up in life to notice our absenteeism. We knew that in a wink of an eye it would all be over. We would each have our own kids, husbands, jobs and general American dream bull-shit to deal with, so, we took the moments when we could. It was great. Anyway, we headed out to the corn fields to get lost for awhile. I loved being in the corn fields. They made me feel short like the other girls. Small and waif. I was five foot ten since I was 14 years old. Most girls my age were small and willowy. My best friend Nichole used to tell me I was a combination of Isabella Rossellini and Julia Roberts. Not bad for a girl in the early 90's. However, most guys were half my size and put you in mind of Tom Petty or Dwight Yoakum. Enough said. Long unkempt hair and big horsy teeth to fit my big horsy mouth that used to get me in trouble, regular, with my old man. We all had the same problem. Our parents couldn't believe we didn't want to spend the rest of our lives in panty hose and heels working for "the man" or working the till at the local Giant Eagle with kids strapped to our sides. Go figure. Those days were our only escape. Even though we knew that particular future was inevitable as long as we stayed in Youngstown Ohio. THAT was our future.

As I said before, the corn stalks rose above our heads and we laid on the damp cold ground and stared into the autumn sun. Smoking pot and drinking and dreaming. Each one of us with a dream to do more than our parents had. Each one of us with a pregnancy scare behind us at seventeen years old. Each one of us with a dream. The sky was a bit gray with the sun amber and warm fighting through the blanket of cold. I lied there for hours just listening to the other girls talk. About men, life and sex and drugs and rock and roll. I could smell the earth underneath my body and I shivered from the chill but dare not move. It was too beautiful and too nice and too safe. We started laughing thinking about being career women in a just a few months. Laughing about being Melanie Griffith in "Working Girl". I know I wanted to go to New York City. We all did. Hell, Cleveland even. The Little Kings were so warm on my throat and the Newport cigarettes were just going down the throat so smooth and easy. I was in my bliss. We all were.

Time got away from us. The booze and pot got the best of us. The day was slipping away and turning into night. We stayed. Neither of us hungry. Neither of us with a pager. Neither of us missing. Nichole started telling storied of parties we had at her house while her parents were away on one of their many vacations to Vegas. I could have smacked her when she told the story of me taking off running down Mahoning Avenue in my bare feet screaming. I laugh to myself like it's ancient history. It was my first trip with purple microdot. My buddy, Gene, who drowned last summer in the quarries, chased after me and calmed me down. Talked me through the whole scene. My mind separates for a moment trying to remember his face. His smell and his sound. I knew, at 15, that I was supposed to meet him. I allow my mind to wander into the future…fantasy future, that if he had lived, we would be together. Eighteen does that to you. Allows your mind to go THERE. I'm snapped back to reality. I have to pee and it is so dark that you could only see each other when someone flicks' their bic. Laughing, I run for the cutlass and turn the key. I turn the brights on and jump in the car. The radio is jamming and the dome light stays on. I throw the car in reverse and park it angled at the corn field to shed a little light on the girls. I jump out and let the music play so that we can each find a collective corner to run to, to relieve ourselves. What a dream. Caught in a corn field with our pants down. I can hear the cops telling my father now. It's about this time that we realize we are out of drinks and almost out of cigarettes. Sucks. Amy and Maggie pull out some shit and we do a couple of rails to "just straighten out" enough to drive back to the school so everyone can get their cars and head home. It was the times. Enough said.

Smelling like we spent the day in the barn and pulling dirt and hay from our hair, we climb into the car. I remember yelling at everyone to shake off so that my powder blue interior doesn't get destroyed. I laugh about that now. Nichole takes the driver's seat and I ride shot gun in my own car. The usual. We decide she should stay at my house tonight. The usual. We drop the girls off at the Mahoning County Career Centre. We take the short winding dark ride to my father's house. We put the car in park and make a plan to say hello and sneak past my grandmother. (My father worked the evening shift at the plant. No worries from him tonight.)

We enter my house from the garage. My grandmother is sitting in her worn light brown lazy boy. Waiting for me. We give our greetings and salutations and I wave Nichole onward and upward to my room. My grandmother circles me and whispers (not sure why) that I smell like I've been in a "beer garden" all night. I smile. She tries to feed us. I smile and reject the food and explain that I'm bushed from studying all day. I make up some story about Nichole fighting with her parents and back out of the room.

Lying in bed that night, waiting for sleep. I know I will never have those days again.

But, with eyes closed, and maybe some good grass to help me along, I feel it come over me again. Once more.

The Bus

The putrid stink of old deep frying oil permeates the air. Why? Every time I'm on the bus hung-over. Going to work. Running errands. This. This is the smell that I smell.

I jump on the 18 headed for the village. I gotta run some errands and get my ass back home. I got one day off and I'm planning on making the most of it. You know what I mean?

My ass feels too big for this seat. I got a pristine white Canadian twenty-something sitting next to me. I like to make her feel uncomfortable. I edge her towards the window a little more. She's a student, she can handle it. I laugh to myself. We may be the only Caucasians on this bus. Again, I laugh to myself. She tries to look out the window and acts like I've attacked her or something just because I've entered her air space. Could be worse, baby. Could be worse.

Fuck the clock

Tick tock

Tick tock

Tick tock from the north country

Tick tock, baby

Where the snows lay long

Everything freeze

Everything cold

I wonder if they remember me at all?

Does time freeze?

In the cold.

And, the brightness of the winter sun?

Leaves twist and burn under the weight.

Trees sigh like angels in the wind.

But,

We are beautiful here.

We are beautiful here.

My cigarette smoke hangs like my own personal cloud.

A halo in the dark atmosphere.

But,

We are beautiful here.

I wonder if they remember me at all.

There was a time I would pray.

They would still love me.

Need me.

Want me.

Remember me.

In the brightness of my day.

I pull my coat tight around my chest and neck.

Walking down Corydon Avenue,

I know this is it.

This is all there is.

Lighting another cigarette,

I watch the halo form.

The stop sign has ice covering it and making it ethereal.

I ignore its' message and keep moving.

February in Winnipeg.

Fuck the clock.

How do I feel?

How does it feel,

Once you've laid your hands upon me?

And, showed me who you are?

I've listened with feminine good manners.

I've laid still.

I've "behaved".

I thought I was mistaken.

Now, bloodied, bruised and humiliated.

You've shown me who you are.

Leave me.

Before I've grown too cold.

And, lose my north-east Ohio, polite, upbringing.

And, show you who I am.

42

I sometimes think I need to start starving my body again.

You know?

Stop eating again.

Work out into some oblivion.

Let the endorphins take over.

I have always felt better when my body is needy and starving.

Too thin and weak for actual conversation.

(Or thought.)

Never "officially" diagnosed.

I've just accepted it.

Sometimes, I get over it and allow the natural plumpness of my heritage to take over.

But, then.

But, then.

I can't take it and the "other" feelings take over.

I thought that turning 42 would change this.

It doesn't.

I still see the same images in the magazines.

I still hear the same messages.

It calls to me like an old friend.

The emaciated Christ on the cross.

Eddie in a Warhol film.

Patti, belting out GLORIA.

Mick, prancing on stage.

You feel me?

Just when you thought it was over, baby.

Here it comes.

Again.

Start me up.

Is that bad?

(I laugh to myself)

Somethings do not get fine with age.

I should erase this whole passage.

But, karma dictates I don't.

Trust the process, people.

Trust the process.

Master of my own domain.

I blame the remaining catholic in me that years have been unable to exorcise.

Enough said.

Anima

I is ugly.

My eyes are too big for my face.

(Natalie Wood, no, sir)

My lips are full and chapped.

My hair is bush thick.

My jaw is square and thick.

(Like my dearly departed uncle Bobby)

I am tall.

(5'10")

I am built like a brick shit house.

Hour glasses are fashioned after me.

I am beautiful.

I'm going to take you down.

There are continents that would celebrate.

There are continents that would shun.

But, I am.

I am.

Act like I don't remember

My sister acts like she just doesn't care.

Everything haunts us.

Our dreams are not alive.

Or something worse.

We was raised to believe that all was good. And whole. And just.

It wasn't.

My sister found heroin.

I found food and booze.

My parents loved us as best as they could.

But, we were.

My younger sister died.

She died before she could remember.

Before she could know the difference.

Call it another lonely day.

Everything has changed.

Everything has shown itself in the sun.

Naked.

Lonely as the day we was borne.

My sister has hep C and broken relationships that span the country.

Children.

I have my "addictions" and predispositions to religions, politics and relationships.

But, we is American.

Born and raised.

From hard-working, Youngstown, Ohio.

Happy and delusional.

People look but, they don't stay long.

Just gawkers.

It's a weight.

But, the devil walks side by side.

He grins and waves his wings.

Beats in time to the heavy steps of our feet.

Life goes on.

What would Hemingway say?

You give yourself away.

You become.

You become the things.

The person.

The person that you think everyone wants or expects.

You give yourself away.

We are all borne into this.

We are all right and we are all wrong from the beginning.

We become an amalgamation of whatever our parents are.

I never tried to be my father.

But, I was and am him.

Everything that we learned happened before we were ten years old.

Our behaviors.

Our views.

Our intellect.

We ran with what we knew.

We ran.

Method actors, all of us.

Give me what I need.

TO FEEL.

TO SCREAM.

TO LIVE.

The bus is late.

I act like everything is all right and move on into the beautiful day.

You touch me in that place.

I act like I wanted you too.

Seeing the world in green and blue.

I feel the pine needles and snow crush under my weight.

It's a beautiful day.

Take me to that other place.

Make me real.

Isn't that what you wanted to hear?

Isn't that what you wanted to feel?

Isn't that what you wanted to see?

And, with every little act.

A bigger piece of me dies.

What would papa say?

Untold

I say I want my story to be untold.

Keep it with me.

Forever to hold.

A mystery.

Unjudged.

For me to hold.

A diamond ring never to be pawned.

A promise I made.

But, all I want is you.

My love will work out and last you throughout the night.

But, my story will be untold.

Johnny

Sitting in the little corner of my basement apartment kitchen, I sit on my 1980's era wheelie chair facing my laptop. All the motivation and intention to write the next FOR WHOM THE BELL TOLLS, only to meet my old friend....nothing. Nothing is an old man with long gnarly fingernails, sour alcoholic breath and a bad heart. He has long white hair with single strands of black intertwined in his very long loose braids. He wears a beat up rust colored robe (thread bare). He has the same sense of humor as Hawkeye from MASH. Smart-assed old man with a hoarse voice and a nicotine laced laugh. He mocks me and he loves me. He sits at my left side and pokes me in my ribs when I start to drift or if I start to focus and begin to write. He asks me to call him Johnny. Okay. "Okay, Johnny, leave me alone. I'm a writer god damn it. I'm a fucking artist. I'm a creator. I'm a god damn intellectual. You are interrupting fucking brilliance."

Johnny sits next to me on the bus when I am running errands, going to work or at home watching television. He makes me feel so masochistic. Johnny likes to watch daytime television. Cops, robbers, child rapists, drug addicts, Kardashians and self-help fucking television psychologists. My father and mother tell people that "I was such a normal child". "She was always a bit rambunctious, but such a creative spirit." "She started reading and writing and drawing at such an early age. She passed her older sister up in school, even though she spent so much time off school from pneumonias and ear infections. A very sickly child. A very smart child. A very normal acting child. She had so much energy. It was palpable. Even from her sick bed. But, "normal"." I would give voice to inanimate objects. Like cotton balls and stuffed animals to entertain myself and my sisters. To bring a smile to worried faces. Johnny was never around. He didn't exist until recently. He was birthed through adolescence. It was a breach birth. Bloody and painful. I shook Johnny off many a time throughout my life. I would discover people, places and things. He would disappear. When I first got married and became a mother. When I got a regular 9-5. When I became responsible and became the regular folk. Johnny put on his rust colored robe and walked into my life like he owned it. He handed me my remote control. He handed me my rye bottle. He handed me my union card. He handed me my mortgage. He handed me my credit card bills. He handed me my tax file. He handed me my passport. He handed me my social insurance number. He handed me my daughter's school principal. He handed me my younger sister's death. He handed me my family members' illnesses. He handed me my self-doubt. He handed me the brick wall that separates me from myself. "Merry fucking Christmas, Johnny! And, I didn't get you anything."

I tell Johnny to "do one" and promptly put "ROCK AND ROLL AND ROLL ANIMAL" by Lou Reed on my record player.

Forgetting yourself for awhile

I feel my spine slip. My left hip and leg twitch under the weight of my right. My fingers get numb. I can feel my throat loosen. I light another cigarette and pour another drink. (Let it happen. Let yourself give in.) Giving up control, my mind flashes pictures. Photographs of things that have happened and are going to happen. I hear the voices of those who have left me and who remain. I think of the uncle I never met and his parents whom I loved. I think of my sister in the earth of Youngstown, Ohio. I think of the snow of Winnipeg. I think of all the books I want to read and that I want to write. I think of all the original music in my head and the paintings I have yet to create.

Gene

Gene was my rock n roll crush. He had big brown eyes, like a camel. Long black lashes. His nose was crooked from some break as a child. His sister, Mary-Elizabeth, his polar opposite. Quiet and unassuming. He always smelled of Marlboros and Stetson cologne. Long dark auburn hair. Faded black concert t-shirts and a yellow comb in his back pocket. He was nineteen when I was sixteen. Gene was dating my sister and every other female in our school system. His mother died of cancer and he and his sister were living with their step-father. A much older staunch educator of the mentally disabled. Gene would sneak through the basement window of my mother's house to party with my older sister and me. I would try to be cool while my heart would pound in his presence. It was unbearable. He continued to come over and party with me after the clandestine break up between he and my sister. We would walk the streets for hours and smoke pot. He would lament over his mother's passing and my sister's unfaithful heart. He would wait at the bus stop and mean-mug the boys who were harassing me on the bus. He would be the shoulder to cry on when my mother didn't come home from the bar or my father angered me, again. He would breathe fire from his mouth to make me laugh. (gasoline and a zippo) Or sit on the counter of my teenage kitchen and try to catch grapes in his mouth that I threw. He would always tell me Pink Floyd's WISH YOU WERE HERE was our song. When I needed pot or beer, Gene was there. Gene would show up at parties that my best-friend and I were at, just to see what was going on. Gene introduced me to Led Zeppelin, the Doors, Pink Floyd and many other classic rock greats. Never dating anyone after my sister, he moved to Houston with an aunt. There was a year with no Gene. Nichole, my best friend, and I moved through the parties and festivals and the meetings, waiting. On a fall day we drove passed his child hood home and there he was. Waiting outside for a friend. We hugged so tight I could feel the air leave my body. I was eighteen and he was twenty-one. I announced that I was seeing my future baby-daddy. Gene, in true form, dramatically announced that he wanted to meet him. To check him out. Gene proclaimed that his gut told him that my boyfriend wasn't good enough, that he felt it. Finishing his cup of coffee, he climbed the tree in his front yard and proclaimed his love for life. We made arrangements to meet on the following Friday night. Only after him announcing that if I wasn't married by twenty one, he wanted to marry me. In a relationship, I laughed and played with my hair. I gave him a big hug and told him that I would phone him on Friday and proclaimed loudly that if I didn't see him on Friday, I would meet him in Hell. My future baby daddy and I were fighting that Friday evening. I never phoned Gene. He went to the quarries with some mutual friends to party. Gene jumped into the water for a swim and drowned. I saw him a week later in his coffin, with a pack of Marlboros in his shirt pocket and smelling of Stetson cologne. His eyes closed and his lashes thick and black and long. A small smile on his lips. I have dreamt of Gene through-out the years. Always waking, straight up in bed, laughing out-loud.

Conversations with no meaning

Seriously!

I watched a documentary about the topic. F. Scott Fitzgerald influenced Ernest Hemingway, with his book THE GREAT GATSBY, to write a novel. Thus, THE SUN ALSO RISES was borne. I shit you not. It's actually documented that he was semi-jealous of Fitzgerald and told him to stop wasting his talent with drink. I'm paraphrasing, of course. Why are people so shaken to their very core when they find out their heroes or mythical legends were, in fact, just humans?

There are modern day talents in writing. I just prefer to read the ex-patriots of the 1920's. They speak to me for some reason. I've had my fill of zombies, vampires and the malaise of modern day authors who are stuck in some politically correct flu of politically correct rights, regulations and general bull-shit. That's not to say that there isn't any modern talent out there. It's just not to my liking. And, why is that a crime? (Lights another cigarette and shifts the phone to her left ear.) "No, I didn't say that. Or, at least, that's not what I meant. It's a personal preference. I don't dig or get into spy mysteries or movies about super heroes. I want to watch things and listen to songs about people. It's not my fault that most of what I like doesn't exist in 2016. Right? Listen, if that's what you dig, then go for it. Let your freak flag fly! Is what I say. I'm not trying to judge. But, why do I have to defend my own thoughts or feelings? Why should you or I have to be on the defensive about what we like or don't like? (lighting another pal mall menthol, she coughs and laughs nervously.) Listen, change the subject because I can hear the timber of your voice has changed. Seriously."

I'm actually feeling okay. Physically. I think my thyroid bull-shit has calmed down. My left eye is still a little more prominent than my right. But, fuck, that's better than it has been. I'm still taking thyroid meds every morning. It sucks but, it's what I have to do. I guess. I sometimes feel like throwing caution to the wind and stop taking the meds all together. But, I am gutless and afraid of what other physically altering bull-shit it would cause. How about you? No, I really do believe in diet and exercise. My 94 year old grandmother still does joint rotation exercises from her bed before she gets up in the morning. I believe in it. A body in motion, stays in motion. A body at rest stays at rest (laughs at this brilliant statement and fixes another rye and ginger). I don't know what I'm actually feeling, sometimes. My left hip is in perpetual gnawing ache and my chest is killing me. Kind of like I have a rib or something out of place. It's weird. But, I can tell it's muscular and not a heart attack (laughing out loud and lighting another cigarette). I have noticed that my breath is weird. Kind of smells like urine. And, my teeth feel like they are somehow suspended. Or, floating in my head (laughing uncontrollably silencing the ice cubes in her glass). Oh and, a distinct taste of black licorice in my mouth. Weird. I hate licorice. Black or red. Kind of reminds me of rubbing alcohol or absinthe. Which I don't really mind. (laughing uncontrollably). Oh, really? When did they find that? A mass in the bladder? Fuck me. That can't be good. On any level. So, what are they going to do about it? Fucking doctors. Love 'em but wish we could live without 'em. Hey? Fuckers. Well, may the gods be with him. I'm sure everything will be okay. There are a ton of new advances in medicine. Friggin' amazing shit these days. But, let me know if you need anything. Truly. Not sure what I can do from Canada, but, let me know. I'm there. (Fixing another drink, she notices the dust on the TV and the beads of sweat on her upper lip.)

Why is it every time I talk to someone from home I get nervous? Never good news. Fuck.

Sorry. I lost concentration for a minute. What did you say? Oh, okay. I thought you said something else (laughing and staggering slightly to the left.). To be honest, I'm not at all interested in American politics. Yes, I'm a citizen by birth but that's about it. I'm not at all embarrassed to say that. I actually don't identify with Canadians, either. I'm actually not sure where I belong. (laughing and pacing the living room floor). I guess if I had to cast a ballot it would be for Sanders. Yes, I'm female and American and expected to vote for Clinton, but I would go Sanders. Although, I'd love nothing more than to see a Jew and a woman in the white house (cackling laugh that goes on a few too many seconds) I find myself as the 'token American' at work. It's an accepted form of bias to hate Americans. I don't really say too much. I was always raised to believe that politics and religion are not work topics. For some reason I find that I am asked some of the dumbest questions. I choose to ignore them. This way I keep my friends and my job. I actually told my daughter not to readily make available the fact that she is an American. For her safety. And, yes, it is shocking, considering we are in Canada."

Um, yes, I love Lebanese food. Really? It made you sick? Maybe, it was the spices. Hey? Sometimes you never know what is going to hit the belly, hard. I pretty much eat to live. Nothing gourmet or too simple. Just eat. Eating shouldn't be so complicated. Hey? Just eat what you like and pay penance when you have to. As I age, I learn what will put me in the can for hours and what will allow me to move into my day swimmingly. (She picks the scar on her chin and tucks her hair behind her ears. Shifting the phone to her right ear and continually pacing. Her left toes start to ache and she sits crossed legged on the sage green couch. Hunched over like a defeated warrior, part of the conversation. Part of the outside world.)

Absinthe

I bought a bottle of absinthe when I self-published my first book of poetry. I was waiting for the liquid jewel to soothe my soul. I wanted the pearl milky liquid to make me feel free. There was nobody singing to me. There was nobody "freeing me'. I watched the emerald liquid glow from the small glass with sugar cubes suspended over my "special' spoon as water was gently poured. I didn't feel like Hemingway. I didn't feel like Fitzgerald. I didn't feel like me. I didn't feel. It didn't change my violence. It didn't change the chatter in my brain. It didn't change.

You know, Dad?

60 days ago, you were my dad.

The cops restrained your violence.

(The violence in your head.)

Four-point restraints and meds.

That ain't cool.

And, I'm standing there under your flag.

Standing free.

They are never going to find you.

I'm never going to find you, dad.

You are nobody's patsy anymore.

You is free.

You is free.

And, the sky burst with colour and wept.

It wept for you and your life.

And, the cold white tiled floor gave way.

Revealed the true nature of your brain.

No more your dirty word.

Standing under your flag.

Free in four-point restraints.

But,

You is free.

You is free.

With the lights out,

You are less dangerous.

Child

The pain behind my left eye throbs in time with my heart.

I feel the rigid muscles in my neck and arms and chest.

Nothing taste the same.

Nothing sounds the same.

Nothing feels the same.

Nothing is the same.

I am nowhere.

Tick tock tick tock

Life is cruel.

To be a child again.

To not know the things that I know.

I was walking ahead of my father through the tall grass in the autumn sun burned clearing. Making racket to flush out the pheasants. My sister is to my right. Complaining about mud. The sun is beating down on my stocking covered head. My cheeks are flushed and my toes are cold beneath my yellow snoopy rubber boots. I am wearing my small orange vest proudly and clumsily fingering the empty dark red rifle casings in my pocket. My breath is heavy and circles from my mouth upwards into the grey sky. Singing songs from the sound of music at the top of my lungs to scare the birds from their nests, my father strolls a few feet behind in his flannel shirt and bright orange vest. The rifle in his arms is brown and grey, metal shining in the sun. The grass is tall and meets my waist. I imagine being in the amazon jungle cutting down foliage looking for an ancient lost treasure. Then, a bird flies into the sky. Small and brown and flapping his wings in a hurry to reach the grey sky. My father cries out "Get down!" I drop to my belly, kissing the earth and a shot rings out vibrating my ears and my body. Lying there, I smell the earth. I breath deep and I smell the earth. My father reached his hand to me. I looked up in fear. Shaking off the grass I choke back my fear and stand tall next to him. The three of us walked side by side through the field. Finding the wounded rooster pheasant, I stand staring at the eyes of the bird. Still gleaming and moist. My father reached down and placed the bird into his old red gunny sack. I carried the sack the whole way to the car. I could smell the gun powder and blood. Holding tightly to the sack, I rode the whole way home. Silent, stroking the feathers and tasting the salt of my tears. Quietly mouthing a prayer to my catholic mother.

Cumbersome

To be anorexic in mind.

(My body reveals nothing)

Alcoholic by birth.

I want you to notice when I'm not around.

I sing loudly and feel every melodramatic note from the guitars.

My voice is not my own.

I cower behind a laptop.

Behind a screen.

My only outlet, is my words.

Feel me.

Breath me.

But,

Never see me.

The devil may care.

And we dance into heaven with his purple highness.

I dream of Paris and San Francisco.

I drink until I am blind.

I exercise until I am exhausted.

And,

You never notice when I'm not around.

I am an adult woman who fights off human beings for a living.

I am Freud's text.

I am me.

You don't grow out of my conditions.

You don't leave my conditions.

If I knew my way out.

I would without breaking your heart.

You gave it to me freely.

Allowing me to take you apart.

(melodramatic guitar solo)

Don't mistake my kindness for weakness.

If you stick around long enough,

(And pay attention.)

I will show you who I am.

But,

Will we understand?

And, I meditate to the universe asking for forgiveness.

And, I ask for peace.

But,

You should know…

You look great when I am high.

I think I know how you feel.

Desperation is a tender track

Your love is diaphanous

I am naked, attempting to cover myself from the world.

Blinding myself from the truth.

Hiding my head in the cliché of sand.

Wrapping my cold limbs in the sky's storm clouds.

My mind is cold steel.

My heart is beating.

My breath mocks me.

I am tired.

I hold the secrets you don't want anyone to tell.

I give you absolution.

I drink another glass of wine and ask the same for myself.

My mind is cold steel.

My heart is beating.

My breath mocks me.

PTSD/DEMENTIA

(and all things bad)

I left and never looked back.

Or so I thought.

I kind of wear the place in my clothes.

It lingers on you.

Like cigarette smoke.

Never really leaving.

Always there.

Can you smell it?

I always knew something wasn't quite right with him.

But, I loved him.

I accepted him.

(For who he was)

I played around and joked when he wanted to.

I listened to his stories even though I knew they were not the truth.

I laughed when he laughed.

I cried when he cried.

I accepted the physical blows.

I learned to heal.

I accepted the emotional roller-coaster.

And, I stood by his side.

I cleaned him up when he needed help doing so.

I helped him eat when he couldn't do it on his own.

And, I cried when he didn't know he was supposed to.

I loved when he didn't know he was supposed to.

I apologised.

I argued and fought.

I cried when he didn't know he was supposed to.

I loved when he didn't know he was supposed to.

Can you smell it on me?

And, all of it is his and mine.

It is all his and mine.

Dad

Who would have known how bitter-sweet this would taste?

Sometimes I pretend that I am someone else.

That the things that I remember happened to someone else.

(It wasn't me.)

But, the physical memory hurts.

It is mine.

It is yours.

Where do we go from here?

How do I make it better?

How do I ease my pain and "fix" yours?

When will it finally go away?

I tried to meet you.

To heal myself.

To hopefully hear something that would ease my soul.

But, the miles are too great.

The words are not there.

But, I am sorry.

You will never hear this.

Even if you do, you won't remember.

It will never tare you apart anymore.

But, I will.

I will burn.

Nothing will ever be said to ease me into the future.

Nothing will ever repair us.

It is.

I will try.

But, the loneliness is for both of us.

And, I can't live with or without you.

I promise, I will love you from the outside.

No Service

I pour another rye and ginger as I turn on my music. I pick PURPLE RAIN and turn the volume up. I shut the windows and light a cigarette. (Don't want the neighbors to hear my "19th Nervous Breakdown") At 43, I figure I've sang and choreographed to this soundtrack for a couple of decades. Without reason or a care in the world I move and laugh and sing and dance. I sweat out the bad. I sing out the bad. I let the tears flow. I laugh like a lunatic at the sun, moon and stars. I give the finger to heaven and hell. I get breathless and loose. My cell phone loses service when I sit in this part of the basement. The universe at work for me? Probably. I take the moments that mean nothing and everything. I paint masterpieces in my brain and I write the next great American novel. I take care of family and love my husband all in the duration of nine songs. I hit repeat and practice my dance moves. I cover my ear phones with my hands and hit the high notes and I imagine that I am as free and careless as I was at ten years old. The sound track has changed throughout the years, the beverage and the reason as well, but the goal has always been the same. I raze myself and begin again. AND, at that time…there is no service.

Indigo

I am nowhere. Where there are no rules.

I feel cruel.

My chest hurts and my finger tips are numb.

I am blue.

I would kill a cricket should it pass by me right now.

Just for crossing my path.

Just for singing it's song.

I feel cruel.

My conscious screams to me.

My hands are tied.

My heart is racing and I try to cover the fevered look on my face.

I am told that in love there are no rules.

My limbs bubble and itch.

I am nowhere. Where there are no rules.

I am blue.

My conscious screams to me.

I am told that in love there are no rules.

I am nowhere. Where there are no rules.

I am blue.

You told me you were fading

I can't remember if I took my meds today. But, I can tell you haven't.

I see you, so thin.

I see you pissing in the corner of the room.

Talk. Talk. Talking.

About?

What, I don't know.

I ask if you know who I am.

"Yes."

(With a smile.)

You ask me where my father is.

I tell you, "right here."

Even in my dreams, I can feel the weight.

Nana

My last photo of you is in your purple shirt.

We talked about life.

"words of wisdom"

I begged a God, I'm not sure that exists, to take you in your sleep.

(your request)

And he did.

Now, I want you back.

I want to tell you what you mean to me.

I want to thank you for never breaking down in front of me.

I want to thank you for letting me take care of you.

I want to thank you for being a part of my life.

I just want to thank you.

Thank you.

Whiskey Bar

I was perverted and diverted.

It came easy.

No one ever noticed.

(not even me.)

I look at my windows.

My floor and my ceiling.

I look all around and never move.

I am still.

I am still.

I am still here.

COCKSUCKER BLUES

July 10 2013

So, it's another day off with a raging summer-time virus. Brought to my knees with a fever and an inability to eat and dependent on fluids, I find myself sequestered to whatever the television and the internet can nourish my burning brain with. I find the universe works in mysterious ways (excuse my clichés). Bored to death of fever and feelings of malaise, I set myself to find something (anything) that would cause me to have to sit upright for a few hours to ease my aching hips and back from the many hours of sleep I've become accustomed to in the last 48 hours. The internet & the Rolling Stones.

I guess I should start by sharing my earliest memories of the Rolling Stones. I was three years old (1976) and being babysat by my second cousin, Maria. She wrangled myself and my four year old sister to her attic bedroom whilst my parents and extended family made home-made Italian sausage on the main floor below. I was scolded and sent away for being a bit too curious and handling the salt water soaked intestines waiting to be filled. Fun. Maria had a poster of a man on her very angled walls and I remember being mesmerized by the picture. At three I couldn't tell if it was a guy or a girl but I found him pretty and interesting. I remember asking Maria who was in the picture. She laughed and was shocked I'd never heard of him. (Maria, I was three.) Mick Jagger. Need I say more? From that point on I remember having my first real crush or fascination. It is really funny, to even be able to understand or conceptualize such a thing. None the less, that is where it all began and that is where the truth lies. She pulled out a little suitcase looking record player and began to play a collection of 45s, for my sister and I, and I was hooked. For the rest of my life, I always refer to that day (that moment) as my deluge into rock and roll.

Obviously, my taste in music was influenced by my formative years. I grew up with parents and grandparents who loved music. There was always a radio or a record being played. It was great. I heard Motown, Elvis, The Who, Abba, big band, country and disco…I don't believe there was a genre ignored within the first ten years of my life. I consider myself a very lucky girl. A couple of years later we had cable television and I could rely on MTV and HBO to fill in the proverbial gaps for me. What a great time to be a kid. No? I remember seeing a Stones video and being obsessed. My mother remembers me standing in front of the television in a complete and total stare. Um, the video? Mick in a sailor suit and bubbles surrounding

77

the band and filling the room? Sound familiar? I laugh when I think of how weird (for lack of a better word) the whole thing was. In the day and age of" new –wave" 80's plastic and neon, I was still foraging through cedar boxes of LPs and 8 tracks trying to find something that really did something for me. By the grace of the universe, I had neighbors and friends who were excited to share their collections with me. What does this have to do with cocksuckers and the blues? Give me a minute. Allow me to reminisce.

Okay, here we go. Having just shared a trip down memory lane, I thought I had seen, collected and pretty much heard everything (and more) than I ever needed to know about the Rolling Stones. How wrong can one almost 40 year old woman be? Pretty wrong. Thanks to the internet and a raging fever, I am now able to see (in part) the documentary that has gone unknown and unseen, to me, until today, COCKSUCKER BLUES. To be fair, in part, on the incredibly weird YouTube. I didn't know this film even existed until my aforementioned fever driven foray into the internet and the old haunting memories of the Rolling Stones. As I don't believe in coincidence, (thank you, Carl Jung) I feel my vodka and o.j. fever was on a quest. After watching the 1970 GIMME SHELTER documentary, I found a three part (cut up) version of COCKSUCKER BLUES. I watched all three ten minute segments and only after started researching the nature and wonderment of the footage I experienced. Interesting, to say the least. Apparently it is a `movie` that The Stones are currently trying to squelch. Only brought to the forefront due to their latest tour. After 50 years of touring, the documentary is back.

Cocksucker Blues is an unreleased documentary film directed by the noted still photographer Robert Frank chronicling The Rolling Stones' North American tour in 1972 in support of their album Exile on Main St.

-Wikipedia

Um, at this point I am only sighting Wikipedia so that you can begin your own investigation in the above mentioned documentary. I`m still not sure why this documentary would continue to be a source of embarrassment to the band. After all of the biographies and interviews available on the internet, bookstores, hangers-on trying to make a buck, ect. I just don`t get it. I have to say, there was nothing THAT shocking. It only solidifies that The Stones were a product of their time. They were gods and everyone wanted a piece of them. Sure there was drug use and debauchery, there still is today, with most bands. Either way, enjoy the controversy. Check it out if you get the chance. Will it change your point of view, I doubt it. No more than the documentary GIMME SHELTER or the autobiography LIFE. It`s not about being `rock n roll cool` or glorifying drug use…it just is. I guess, all I am trying to say is…when the music, memories and nostalgia have all reached the end, they ARE, just men. Right?

Until the next fever, have a good one.

Andy

I got a white acoustic guitar.

I named her Andy.

(After Warhol)

She is teaching me "Desolation Row".

I am easy.

I wear my lace and put my hands in my back pockets.

I bat my heavy mascaraed eyes.

I sit on the broken down couch and hold Andy.

I lean close to her neck and strum her strings.

(to feel her vibrations)

My husband sits opposite and gets ready for the show.

On my 43rd birthday, I feel Andy sing in my hands.

Waiting for the flood and the eventual rainbow.

I know I'm no good.

So, does everyone who can hear.

I recite psalm 23 and finger Andy.

I am trying to blow it up.

I lean my head and begin to sob.

Nobody is escaping.

Hold your flowers.

Throw them later.

When I'm gone.

Greasy

You got diamonds on your finger nails.

You wait for them to throw loonies on stage.

Even if the sun refused to shine.

You are there.

Tiny dancer, you is 45 years old.

Your daughter phoned and wants you to come home.

Are you going to work tomorrow?

I'll phone and tell them you are sick.

(again)

She needs you to sign her permission slip.

(I forged it for you.)

You should go home.

You should know that she is still loving you.

Go home.

Go home, girl.

Go home.

Take the checks.

Take the checks cuz it's easier.

It's easier, girl.

Dada dada

Hot

Hot like Manilla

Wooden coffee table

Stained

Rings

Rings

Hot like Manilla

Don't bother me.

Don't bother me

Let me smoke my cigarette and burn.

Smoke my cigarette and hurt.

Smoke my cigarette and burn.

Hot like Manilla.

Save me from myself.

The tables have turned.

Moonlight Sonata

Living for another day.

My nervous breakdown begins.

Every six months.

Always on time.

Like clockwork I obsess with weight.

I am aware of my breathing and my beating heart.

I drink too much and eat too little.

I scream for no reason.

You've lost your right to a point of view.

I paint and write for no reason.

I damn the light and the dark.

I cry and laugh in a single sound.

And, I wait.

I wait for the sun.

I wait for the phone to ring.

I wait for a sign that the cloud has passed.

I wait to see if you are still there.

When you are so sensitive,

It's a long way to fall.

Lie for me and I'll lie for you.

My soul decided to wait.

I am going to sit with you for a while.

I'm going to wait until we can" go" together.

I love you.

I'll pretend that you are right and that all of this is normal.

We watch the seasons change from summer to fall.

The colours of the leaves match my hair, you say.

We talk about things I could never remember.

We eat fried cherry pies and watch the Andy Griffith Show.

I sing Buddy Holly songs with you.

I make my grandmother's sauce for you.

We plan for Christmas.

One day, this will all be faded memory.

For me.

Words

Sometimes, I get this strange feeling in my head.

Like a fever, my cheeks flush and I feel my heart race.

I find it hard to breath.

I'm drowning?

My bones feel mushy.

As soon as it appears, it is gone.

I dream of waking up one day and shaving my head

I am not sure why, but I do. I dream in technicolor. I visit loved ones who are here and who have passed. I am always searching and learning and listening. I put my ear to the ground and wait for the signal. Because, I know that it is there. I know that the answer is there. And, I am ready. I put on Jimi and listen to "Hey Joe." I Pour another cup of coffee and wait. I light another cig and listen. I wait for the message. I watch CNN and become terrified. I contemplate constructing a panic room. I shake in fear and I move on into my work day. Terrified by the Muslims. Terrified by the Christians. Terrified of any religion in general. Terrified by the Whites. Terrified by the Blacks and Latinos and the Asians. I wake every morning and contemplate shaving my head. I pour a cup of coffee and light a cigarette. I change the channel. I climb the steps of my bus and I move into my work day.

Blood

I took the trash out this morning,

There was blood pooling on my back walk.

Something hemorrhaged.

Something might have died.

I think it was my rabbit.

A rabbit that lives under my deck.

She looks into my basement window.

I wave hello every morning.

I haven't seen her today.

There is blood pooling on my back walk way.

I'm not broken.

I flashed back to my bleeding out in my shower after a hysterectomy.

I cried and checked my crotch.

I walked through my back door and I collapsed.

I think my rabbit died or gave birth.

Red, White and Very Blue

It's hard to be the token American in a sea of Canadians.

I'm navigating very carefully where I sit at coffee breaks and for lunches.

I keep my gaze low.

Quiet during political discussions that pop up like brush fires.

On the bus, in the stores and everywhere one goes in life.

They are watching.

The world is watching.

Leaving the room whenever colleagues ponder aloud the state of the "south" and how "something like this" could never happen in this country.

Swiftly exiting the area when the United States becomes the topic of laughter.

I noticed they never survey the room before the jokes start.

I once identified my nationality during the comedic discussion of United States politics.

The response, "It's okay. Some of my best friends are Americans."

Even with my brilliant imagination, I couldn't make this stuff up.

Oh, it's all real. It's an acceptable form of bigotry. It's the norm.

Once I've been discovered, I am expected to answer for Trump, Hilary and any other headline maker that enters my opponents thought bubble.

Gun control

Racism

Killer cops

Health insurance

Muslims

Jews

Hispanics

Lack of cultural Diversity

Birtherism

Cultural assimilation

Immigration

Refugees

Etc.

Etc.

Etc.

There is no comfort and no excuse for the reality show fodder that United States has become.

It may be ugly.

It may be hated.

It may be the butt of every joke that I've heard in the past six months,

But, it is my birth country.

Just like family,

my country has made me red with embarrassment.

White with fear.

And, very blue with deepening sadness.

Just like family, I think fondly of her and wish her all of my love.

Eating Crow

I'll tell you what it means…

When the cosmos give you all of your rational.

When your daughter is in a purely sexual relationship with a man who can give two shits about her on any level.

When your father becomes the child and you become his parent.

When your friends become your enemies.

When you become too weak to fight the good fight.

When you become the minority in the majority.

When you receive the hysterectomy that you've prayed for only to have another organ cause you monthly, nah, daily pain.

When your best friend with maloto children goes on a hateful rant speech about another race.

When your mother proclaims to all that is holy that she hopes you have a daughter just like you.

(Prophetic…I did.)

When you have nephews that you haven't seen since they were babies and they still hate you. Just because.

When you've spent your life defending your personal freedoms of speech, religion and liberty; only to have them taken from you due to millennial political correctness.

When your words no longer have any clout because of your divine luck of being birthed in the most hated country in the world.

When you are not considered an immigrant because you are white and only 2200 miles away from home.

When you order a pizza and it is delivered with everything you wanted and some you didn't; pineapple.

When you took four years of French and still can't get the job you want because you are not "fluent".

When you write, paint and sculpt but are "not quite what we are looking for. It won't sell."

When you still hold the belief that everyone is equal and that we are all "one" and reservations, genocide and war is still on the news every single night.

When you have a pantsuit in your closet, have a strong opinion and are considered a lesbian feminist for doing so. (not that there is anything wrong with that)

When you still take care of your husband and family, work a full-time job and enjoy doing so and are a sell-out in the eyes of the millennial hipster crowds.

When you tried to go to university, not once but twice and had to drop out to "deal" with family obligation and issues.

When your grandmother dies one week after you visited her and your mother nose dives.

When you are at the grocery store with a long line-up behind you and the cashier needs a price check.

When you see pictures of Richard Gere and Duran Duran in 2016.

When you are leaving the bar at 10pm.

When you are compared to Sylvia Plath and all you were trying to do was put the pie in the oven and write what you were feeling.

The list goes on and so do I.

Eating Crow.

Use a fork and a knife.

(Keep tooth picks handy for the pin feathers.)

2000 Something: Glory Days

fontaine fountains frolicking in frothy oceans: kiss me and lie to me about you wanting to be here right now with me without me beside me and inside me: selling ice-cream smiles with tombstone teeth licorice striped soft rice cake like bumming a cigarette from me and kissing me softly through the car window as the light picks up a gleam from your wedding ring opening closing and thinking how dare you come so close took so long when will we meet again when will you buy me a drink when will I be deserved of this, "pure as new york snow" I've got an appetite angry blue and damaged BE the "golden god" of teenage love lust and fantasy know I'm talking about you her and the never had a chance moments of our meeting greeting knowing and demise play the "summer of 69" over and over and buy the late-nite blue plate special and practice Springsteen standards in my home town pretending to be the well-dressed monkey for the organ grinder and his organs ground and grinded and winded you asked me to go home and I said no and he said yes and he pleased his wife with me on his mind and told me about it the next week rewind fast-forward and pause knowing glowing and expecting as I get dressed to go drink until I drown with dollar shot specials and wail and raze against the machine of parenthood responsibility femininity and constitutional love and marriage contemplating if I can do to her what has been done to me with her red high hallo of brassy hair and wide mouth wide hips wild right hook fixing my white slouch socks and cleaning my scuffed Doc's collect my british invasion "molly" well-dressed bff and my sometimes frenemy pulled her car around and I jumped in and I kissed you and bit you and spit and split… you could never look me in the eye and I wasted make-up for this shit.

Pure

It's cool you can lie to me. I get it being an artist and all. We all want to be pure but I've been here before. I've closed that door before. I've opened them too. You can lie to me. Nobody wants to be seen in the gallows and nobody wants to see the chair. You can lie to me. I don't care if you're lying to yourself. I'll never leave you. You can lie to me. I'll be here. I'll be here. You got a problem and I am here. You can lie to me. You got a problem and you can lie to me. I saw the couch and I knew it was monkey business. I turned the straight lines into dotted lines and I went to the store and bought castor oil. I filled my prescription too. I filled your prescription too. I called the "monkey man" and I said I have cash and he said, "No!". I've been to the church and waited in the wooden box. I told the man that I was sorry. And, he said it's okay. He said it's okay. As, I say to you that it's okay. You can lie to me. I'll lie to you. But, I know. I know. I know. You got this girl. That is the only truth. You got this girl. That is the only truth.

THE ONLY TRUTH.

Can I get you a coffee?

Hey

The truth of the matter, no, the fact of the mater is that I just don't care what other people think. There is a distinct difference between the fact and the truth. I walk around with this bad taste in my mouth. I feel like if I yawn or cough, a raven will spill black feathers from my pie hole. Everyone will see it and feel it and know it. Discovered as human. I don't ask for forgiveness or penance. I don't ask for much. Maybe it was more than a lot. Now you've got me crawling to the alter. Carrying the weight of an elephant on my back. Who will carry me? Who will build the boom? Who will give me wings or wheels? Who will speak when I scream in silence? Who will hear for me when I no longer understand? Who will pump the blood through my heart when mine is broken? And who will chew the pablum of your words and swallow them for me? Yes, while you continue to wait for the end of the world, I will drink and think and lead you, he, she, it and them into the garden and I will eat that forbidden fruit and take your rib. And, that is the truth and the fact of the mater.

Toodles

Silly spitting swallowing choking viperous frenemy fuck hell damn bullshit dream master bastards; toodles and doodles to the rest of the bar and this place Winnipeg and Youngstown and all the other map's points of pleasure and deranged thoughts of life as I know it and pretend to know it controlled cut adrift from the life's blood of knowing who I was and would be rain war dancing on the hoods of cars of lovers who have gone by choice and because they were dismissed or missed or pissed and I sing and I wail and I go slow and then fast and pause for the applause until it comes I start again with new shit and a new fever and new aches and new pains and I say it is fear and it is desire that brought me here and I walk and work into the new millennium afraid of the oven's door and the medicine cabinet compared and repaired by the Sylvia factor laughing crying sighing and breathing in a single sound of silence closing that door over and over until there are no rules and I bruise shaken from the very core of blood and bone knowing that we are and always will be the pale dust of the gods' chess board eclipsed sometimes by the sun and secretively whispering into my deaf ear forming the words that I long to hear; you're so cruel.

Little fish, big fish

I walk down the street into the burning trees crisp air bites the back of my throat and I think of them. I feel the sun burn through the outstretched limbs. Lighting another cigarette, I continue on recounting the summer of my smiles. Some things are clear from time to time. Like the burn from the first sip of a really good whiskey or the smell when the furnace kicks on for the first time of the cold season. Backyard bonfires with family and friends. When you first said that you loved me, I watched the fire as it grew so slow. I felt that comfortable burn. I remember getting dressed up in my special clothing to join my grandparents at church for the holidays. Patten leather shoes and skirts. The smell of the church with its frankincense, smoke and mirrors. I feel the coldness of my winter moving in. I am rising and falling in the mystery of my season's change. Cyclic, I feel the blue start to break the amber landscape. Cyclic. Holding tight to my sweater I step on my cigarette and breathe deep the air. The cold beautiful and amber air. It feels good. If I had a voice I would sing.

Wings

I can feel the change in my psyche. I know it is here and it is now. I feel the beating of angels' wings in my inner ear. Flapping, beating and bleating like goats in a cage. I can hear them as life goes on around me. Can you hear them? There is a question in my eyes as I gaze into the mirror. I am 43 and still learning as a wise man and a fool. I can feel the change in my psyche. I am on automatic pilot as I board the bus and go to work. Bathe, feed and walk. I am not living in a vault. I will come and go and speak and have sex and breathe and who really cares? I will defend this and that and all that I cannot see because it is your reality. I am a woman on the move and I know they will sell pictures of my sinking. The festival is in town and it doesn't matter which one it is. Everyone will be there wagging tongues and raising flags. The music of the accordion will rise and fall and the harmonica will scream to interrupt the night. Don't leave. Once the society folk leave it will be clean and good and bright again. We are not expecting rain. Join me for a beer at the festival of fools. The firecrackers break the black sky as I move down the alley into the filth of the forgotten mattresses, couches and appliances. The bags rise like glaciers on each side and the flies party to the night's music. I bum a cigarette from the pimple faced kid too drunk to remember our conversation or that he was even there. I light my smoke and take your arm as we move on into the dark and beautiful night. We know more than they do. We feel the heartache of the streets as our feet take the timing of the accordion music and watch the neon lights fight for time in the night sky with the fireworks. I can't see the moon for the smog and clouds. But, I know it is there. Is it there? I feel your breath change as we move on and we march into the next adventure waiting for Disney to change our views. Waiting for a kiss to wake us from this sleeping reality. I can hear the wings of the angels' beating and bleating like goats in a cage. Can you hear them? When you ask me how I am doing, I think it is a joke. I am ready to go anywhere.

The door is open but the ride ain't free

It is a beautiful sunny day as I exhale the smoke from my lungs. I have to pause and notice the warmth and the blue sky. I can hear the leaves dry and brittle move like ants across the ground. Hurrying, as if they have someplace else they would rather be but beneath me. Near me. I am tired and my ears are ringing. I usually put music on very loud to write. It drowns out the noises of everyday life and allows me to concentrate on my inner thoughts. But, today there is no need. The inner noise is greater than any song I could blare from the speakers. Today, it is louder in my head.

I can hear my mother in law moving around upstairs and for a minute I slip into thoughts of living with my grandmother. She too would move about clumsily through the house making sure that everyone and everything knew where she was. Purposefully? For a moment, I imagine the noises I am hearing are that of my grandmother. I can almost hear her slurping the hot coffee from her over filled mug. I can hear her eating her soda crackers slathered in butter and jam and I can smell her Sanka and skin cream from the other room.

My face is flushed and I'm not sure if it is fever or emotion that burns my cheeks. I am neither sad nor happy. I just am.

It is a beautiful sunny day as I exhale the smoke from my lungs. I have to pause and notice the warmth and the blue sky.

- Hey, sister-luck, can you spare a smoke?

The sweat beads across her upper lip and I notice the front teeth missing. She gives me a pirate's smile and asks me for a smoke. "Sorry, it's my last one. You can have the rest if you want." She grabs the butt and inhales deeply. One hit wonder. She is holding a plastic water bottle with a rag wrapped around it. Drops the smoke and inhales deep the fumes from the rag. Gives me another grin and for a minute I'm reminded of Keith Richards. (No shit) She asks me where I'm going and if I can spare some change. "Sorry honey. Everything is on plastic these days. Must be hard now that this is the new norm. Hey?" She looks at me like I'm from another planet or like I've got lobsters crawling from my ears. She looks like she is my age. Thin limbs and a round middle. Weather worn face. But, kind. Very kind. I can hear the Canadian lilt in her voice mixed with the accent of her people. I know she needs something to hold on to. Someone to listen. Someone to listen too. Maybe just a drink? I sigh to myself and wonder what brought her to this place. Where did all of her ancestors go? Are they sharing smudging ceremonies with mine? Are we the same age? Did we have the same experiences with school, boys, men, religion and music? No. Definitely no. For a minute I want to forget about the suburban humdrum of banking, grocery shopping and "what have you" and take off into the streets with her. Go on a pub crawl and record her every sound. Her every smell. Her dying and her waking. I wanted to drop my white winter coat in the filthy street and say, "Fuck it!" I wanted to know her story and I wanted to know why she called me, sister-luck. I took a couple of paces backwards while her gaze held me steady and reached into my back-pack and found a couple of loonies and a loose smoke. I shook her hand and wished her well. The siren from a fire truck screamed in the distance and she startled and staggered and looked over her left shoulder. I turned and walked into the grocery store. When I came out of the store, she was gone. I put the ham on rye I had bought her into my bag and walked to the bus stop.

He

"Do you like to listen to Leonard Cohen?"

He answered that only when he was feeling blue. I answered, "I like to listen to him all the time. No matter the mood." He looked at me and lit another cigarette. I ordered another G&T from the bartender and took a long sip. I cocked my head to one side and lit a cigarette. "I'm waiting." I say. His long hair covered his eyes from my sight. "Is that somehow a conversation breaker?" "What is your favorite song, and please don't say Hallelujah". He takes a shot of Sambuca and slams the shot glass on the bar and steps back from the bar like he was swallowing fire. I laughed. "That is exactly what I was going to say." He laughs a big wide toothy grin and I notice the discoloration on his front right tooth. It was beautiful. I was thinking of the speech I used to give to my teenage suiters…"I like roses. But, I like them with the thorns still on them. I hate when florists remove them. They become unnatural and ugly then." Nothing has changed in that department. "I prefer people who scream when they burn." he says. "Bukowski. Great stuff." He orders two more shots and sends one flying my way a foot or two down the bar. "You should know I'm spoken for. I have a boyfriend. I'm not sure he will like me accepting Sambuca from strangers. Especially those who don't really care for music, do ya?" I wink and take the shot. I throw my head back and can feel the heat in the back of my throat and the sweet taste of anise fills my mouth. "God, that burned. Hey?" "If your boyfriend wouldn't like you doing shots and talking to strangers, why are you continuing then? Are you breaking chains that you think I can repair?" "Give over mister man. You ain't so mucking fuch." I laughed a good full red headed laugh and moved another bar stool further away. "I think the band is about to start up again and my friend Jamie should be here any minute. Thanks for the drink. Maybe I'll catch you later." "Sure. I'll see you around. Any time." Jamie comes over and we hug and order more drinks. The band starts into their second set and we move on into the night. People were talking and laughing and dancing and the room was a whirl of lights and sound and smell. The band sounded like a carnival in the little paneled walls of the local hole in the wall. Jamie was buzzed and I was buzzed and we didn't have a care in the world. We laughed until our faces hurt and our ears were ringing and our make-up was dripping and we were alive. As the bar keep called "Last call for alcohol." I felt the sadness of the night's end move through me. We waited until the lights came on in the bar and hugged and kissed the band; old friends of ours and staggered out to Jamie's car. I rolled the passenger window down deep in thought and lighting another cigarette and there he was.

"Come over to the window, my little darling. I'd like to try to read your palm. I used to think I was some kind of gypsy boy. Before I let you take me home. So, so long Marianne." He leaned in through the window and kissed me gently.

Love story

He was pushed over the line a long time ago. He gave and shook his ass for all to see. All hangers on. Watching the show. Smiling big toothy grins. Giving everybody everything they ever wanted and it wasn't even what they wanted. I moved in him and he moved in me both desperate and clinging to the one thing that would stop the lies. I screamed and he screamed and accepted the outcome. I wore his love like a crucifix around my pale neck. Clinging to it in the dark hours. He took the piss out of me with just one look. He had nothing. More than nothing. We swore to never become our parents only to become our parents. The dishes were thrown and the flower vase underfoot, he grabs the door and runs through. Screaming, to stay with you I'd have to be crazy. And, he was. And, we were. We loved completely and totally and without absolution. Gypsies in the night's air. When the bruises healed and the bandages were removed, it came down to the knees too worn and painful to bend anymore. We clung to each other and promised to be friends. He remarried and had a child. I remarried and moved to another country. To see you, would break me in two. This is how our story ends.

Slipped

Choking on your alibies and breaking the walls one brick at a time tearing and taring jealous and strong I never I never saw the clock move and I never thought I would see the bright side of this light and this mountain is too high and the road is too long I smell the booze on your breath and the perfume in your hair and I run into the dark streets and the cold hits my cheeks like god like a bullet and I feel the strange move into my brain into my spine and heaven isn't close in this place I scream and I rush around rush around and I think I will stop…I can't stop and I don't now somebody told me you still loved me and I can't let you do that to me to her to him I've got potential to be happy and to be me closing my eyes I see the place I used to live when I was me when I was being when I was whole and when I was young Jesus bent low and whispered in my ear in the air hail Mary and I sit still waiting for someone to save me he looked like Springsteen and I ran into his arms and smelled leather and whisky still running I know I can make it if I take one step at a time while the storm gathers in my veins while the storm gathers in my heart and I close my eyes and breath deep the places I used to live the devil's manna doesn't taste that sweet and the water is bitter and I keep moving and more than I will ever know folds before me in your embrace.

Prayer

my spine feels curved and I am unable to straighten up and to stand as I am hallow boned and a vessel of all that floods my body, mind and soul throwing my arms around the world, Buddha, Christ and anyone else who has an ideology a purpose and a yarn and a barn to sell twisting into shapes and people and things wandering and wondering into the shadows of the new day happy in the solitude of knowing that this is all there is and will ever be cigarette tastes like shit and my hands are tight holding and folding the todays and tomorrows like paper into some origami dove climbing the colors of the sunrise trying to capture the moon by surprise to place into my pocket for a later day to gaze upon the hope of another day gentle reminder of things to come.

Melting Pot

I raze myself every couple of weeks to allow the pain, the happiness and the beauty of life to melt into a pot to ponder to create to sell to be as the gentle reminder that one day I too will be old and unable to do the things that foolish people do my eyes sting while watching old videos of my grandparents and something is caught in my throat as I take another belt of rye the symphony plays in the background of my mind as I prepare for another night of debasing always starting around midnight as I stare into my own reflection from the computers screen forgetting myself and everyone around me just for a moment or two as visceral memories rush into my mind and fingers, pictures and words blurred and erasing the "me" that is the work and the public and I see myself as a ghost some things are clear from time to time when they are not flowing and when the thoughts are too heavy to take I take a deep breath and stop knowing that for now I have time to begin again, for whatever that means.

Vega

It was 1978 as I sat on my dad's lap as we did doughnuts in the ice and snow on the side street in front of my aluminum sided house. We were blowing the transmission of the family car, a Vega. I was getting dizzy as I sat on my father's lap laughing and carrying on as the neighbors and my mother sat in their front yards watching and screaming to stop. I gripped the red vinyl covered steering wheel with my yellow mittens that my grandmother made for me. The yarn was greyed and frayed from playing in the snow and helping my father remove the packed ice and snow from the wheel wells before doing our doughnuts. I could feel the sting of the cold air in my nostrils and see my breath as I yelled and squealed on my father's lap. I remember trying to reach the pedals and just steering the wheels in circles over and over again. The back end of the station wagon was fish tailing and we hit the curbs and bounced left and right. The lights on the dash board flickered off and on in time with our laughter. My old man turned the music up on the radio to drown out the ever growing crowed of onlooker's jeers to our fun. We started to run out of gas and I let go of the wheel as my father took over and drove us to the gas station. I was breathless with nerves and exhaustion and fun as we spilled out of the old Vega and headed into the store. My Dad bought me a candy bar and made me promise not to tell my mother. I climbed back into the car as my father pumped gas. I watched him from the rear-view mirror in his fur hat as he stood there blowing on his hands to keep them warm. Humming to the music on the radio and gobbling up my chocolate bar knowing that we were both going to catch hell when we got home. We did, but I wouldn't have changed a thing about that afternoon. Later that night as we sat around the television watching reruns of Star Trek and UFO, I never thought the day would come that I would ever want to leave that place. I could still smell the gasoline and the cold of the grey sky, ice and snow. Remembering riding in my father's car, the memories come back to haunt me and I wish I could go back and relive those moments with him.

Humanity Contained

I always tell my friends that if you want to really experience humanity, catch a ride on public transit. Strangers grouped and contained like sardines in a flat tin. Bunched so close together that you can smell their personal households on them. Their lover's perfume? Their children's cereal? Their medications or vitamins seeping from their skin? I sometimes think I recognize another person's smell as my own or a product we have both used. Commonality. Recognition. Yet, they don't look like me. They don't sound like me. They don't speak like me. They don't have the same story that I do. They can't feel like I do. (or do they?) Teenagers who don't move for the elderly. Men who race to the open door in front of women, other men and children. Chivalry is dead. The mentally ill and the physically disabled trying to reach for "normalcy". The crying and cursing loud cell phone conversations that we are all forced to be passive participants in. The state of politics discussed by the millennial cognoscenti fresh from university. Solving the worlds crisis one "like" at a time. The refugee crisis paying for a ride downtown one quarter at a time. The drunk looking for a free ride to the next beer garden. The pretty blonde with the coach bag who doesn't seem to have enough change. The woman with the double wide stroller and a five dollar bill in her hand trying to get change from the driver and then the other passengers. All the while we continue to squeeze closer and closer together. In the seats, in the isles and pushed out the back door like a bad birth. The slush and grey snow has made it impossible to see out the windows. Reminds me of the few rides I've been on in the subways of New York. Dark and loud and unable to see or hear the "whatever" we are flying by on the outside of our little sardine can. Moving through the day, we are one. Forced to accept each other's smells and sounds and persons. One little can of sardines about to be opened by another unsuspecting stranger. Our sardine god takes the fares and the bus passes and smiles and greets and takes our little fish asses to our destinations. Carefully observing the outside world for us, navigating the streets and keeping us all safely contained. One stop at a time. Sardines.

"Oh the humanity."

Nicole Nesca was born in Youngstown, Ohio in 1973. She developed a love of music, painting and writing early on and continued that love throughout her adult life. While living in Canada, she completed three works of poetry and prose collected in the anthology piece, KAMIKAZE WHITE NOISE, and another two books of poetry and prose. She has been published in several E-Zines and has been a part of two anthologies.

SCREAMIN' SKULL PRESS

CUTTING EDGE
SPONTANEOUS
STREET-WRITING

Novels, Stories, Poems

TONY NESCA   NICOLE I. NESCA

Manufactured by Amazon.ca
Bolton, ON